THE ADVENTURES OF
ARYA
&
KRISHNA
BETTA FISH

Written by Gabriel Bietz

Art by Ananta Mohanta

Illustrations by Ananta Mohanta
Cover Design by Praise Saflor

ISBN: 978-1-7377955-1-3 (Paperback)
978-1-7377955-2-0 (Hardback)
978-1-7377955-0-6 (Ebook)

Library of Congress Control Number: 2021924272

Printed in the United States

To my wife, Amita-
Without you, life would not
be a wonderful adventure.

1

The Adventure Begins

Once upon a time in Wawona, California, there lived two small betta fish: Arya and Krishna.

Arya and Krishna were curious young fish. Both enjoyed adventure and discovering new places. They wanted to explore the world. They wanted to venture to places where they had never gone before and meet new friends.

Our story begins on a sunny day in June; it was on this day that Arya and Krishna began a new adventure. The betta fish were traveling in the back of a red truck from the pet shop. An old man had bought them, and now they were being delivered to his garden pond. Arya and Krishna didn't know how long it would take to get to the pond, but they were happy to move out of the pet shop. They were thrilled to be on a new quest to find their parents.

Arya looked out the window of the traveling truck. "I can't believe we are finally leaving the pet shop," she said. The water in the fish tank was splashing to and fro as the truck traveled on the bumpy road.

Krishna was curious about their new journey. "What do you think the new pond will look like?"

"We are going to find out soon enough little brother," Arya replied, as a wave of water sprayed out of the tank hitting the truck bed with a splash.

The red truck turned down a country road, hitting multiple potholes along the way. Grass between the tire tracks fanned away the dust kicked up by the wheels. After about ten more minutes, the red truck came to a screeching halt. The brakes hissed and gravel slid from beneath the tires.

Krishna's eyes grew wide as he gazed at the traditional Japanese style house. "Are we there yet?" Krishna asked.

Arya swam to the edge of the glass fish tank and looked out the window. "Yup, I think we've arrived. Hey Krishna, that looks like a minka."

"A what?"

"A minka. A traditional Japanese house, I remember that from watching the Discovery Channel while we lived in the pet shop".

"Minka, uh, well I learned something new today. I wonder whom all lives here?' Krishna said.

"Maybe we will find Mom and Dad here," said Arya.

"I hope we find them, I miss them so much," replied Krishna

The delivery man got out of the truck, walked over to the back and opened the tailgate. He reached in and grabbed the fish tank. The water in the tank swished and sloshed.

"Getting a little turbulent in here!" Krishna huffed.

"Here you go, sir," the delivery man said to the new owner, handing him the tank.

"Oh, thank you, my boy. Here is a tip for your troubles," the old man said. He looked into the tank as he carried it to the Koi Pond. "Well, my little betta fish, I hope you enjoy your new home." He started to pour the water out of the tank and into his pond. The water formed a small waterfall.

"Quick, Krishna, let's ride the wave," Arya said, and they plunged into the Koi Pond. SPLASH!

Both betta fish were pushed by the current to the bottom of the pond. They opened their eyes and looked around. The sun shone through the water. Deep blue shadows from nearby plants waved in the current. It was quiet and peaceful... until Krishna shouted, "Wahoo, let's go!"

He raced between the leaves of the plants. Krishna looked back at his sister and then BAM! He backed up slowly and was face-to-face with another betta fish.

"OUCH. Who are you?" asked the betta fish while rubbing his head with a fin.

"My name is Krishna, little dude. This is my big sister Arya. We just arrived from the pet shop. Boy, am I glad to escape that place. Hey, I am hungry. Where can two betta fish find some grub around here?"

"I'm Blake, and this is Sharktooth. We've been here for months and haven't seen other betta fish in all that time."

"What's up, guys? I never thought we'd run into more betta fish either. Arya and I never saw any other betta fish except for our parents while we were living at the pet shop," Krishna said.

Blake looked around. "Your parents are here, too? Where?"

Arya sighed. "No, those pet shop owners sold our parents. We are going on an adventure to find them."

"Don't worry sis, we'll find our parents. I just know it." Krishna put his fin around her. "This is just the start of our adventure."

Arya picked her head up, "At least no customers will be tapping on the glass of our fish tank anymore. That was so annoying," she said, while beginning to see things on the bright side.

"Yup, you won't have that problem here. Let me tell you a little bit about the pond," Blake said. "The water warms in the morning when the sun shines down, and the evenings are cool with a gentle breeze on the surface. We have plenty of food, and you are both welcome to it. The old man is kind and good to us all."

"Good to us all? Are there other fish in this pond?" Arya asked.

"Oh, but of course," Sharktooth replied. "The koi fish can be found in the deepest part of the pond near the aerator. They're massive fish and not to be trifled with in the least bit."

"Why do koi fish stay in that part of the pond?" Krishna asked.

Blake smiled. "That's where the best food can be found."

2

Big Shadows

Over the next two weeks, Arya, Krishna, Blake and Sharktooth became close friends. They played in the tall water grass plants. They even built a small fortress made from colorful pebbles at the bottom of the pond. It was large enough for them to sleep in it at night. The front was guarded by two large smooth rocks with only a small space between them for the betta fish to squeeze through.

"You can never be too careful." Blake said as he swam out of the fort.

"Quit being such a scaredy-cat. We haven't even seen another fish in this part of the pond." Arya said.

"Blake has always been paranoid after running into those Koi when we first arrived to the pond. We had no idea they lived here," Sharktooth replied.

"How did you guys end up in this pond?" Arya asked

Sharktooth took a deep breath and looked over at Arya "Well, you see, our last owner was the old man's grandchild. One day while she was visiting, she tripped while holding our fish tank and the entire aquarium spilled onto the patio in front of the pond," Sharktooth said.

"Ya, Sharktooth and I were stranded on the rocky patio! We had to flip and flop our way into the pond to survive. We loved the pond from the moment we hit the water. There was no way we were going back in our fish tank," Blake said.

"Wow, you guys got lucky," Arya exclaimed.

Blake turned to Arya. "So what's your story? How did you and Krishna end up in the pet shop?"

"Well, our parents were sold by the pet shop, Blake," said Arya.

Blake looked shocked. "That's so sad! Please continue."

"Krishna and I were very young. We hatched from our eggs in the pet shop. Our parents would laugh and play with us every day. They even taught us how to read. Our Dad was sold first a few months ago. Then our mother was sold this week. Krishna and I knew that in order to find them we had to leave the pet shop. When the old man came to the pet shop we knew that was our chance to leave. We swam back and forth at the front of the tank to get his attention. The next day we were moved to the truck." Arya looked down, "I do miss my parents. Krishna and I think about them all the time. That's why we love going on this adventure. I hope that one day we will find them again."

"We were excited the old man bought us so that we could go out into the world and find them. I always try to keep a positive attitude." Arya said.

Blake put his fin around Arya. "We'll help you find them."

There was a long moment of silence as they swam.

"Where is Krishna?" asked Sharktooth.

"He is taking a nap, I think," Arya said.

At that moment, Krishna woke up and swam out from the rock fortress. "I see you guys are up already. I'm starved!" He swam to the surface to where the old man always sprinkled food, but there was nothing there.

"Guys, did any of you see the old man this morning? I think he forgot to feed us," Krishna said.

"I haven't seen him," Arya said.

Blake and Sharktooth shook their heads. "We haven't seen him, either."

Three days passed and food became scarce. "I am getting a little worried. What if something happened to the old man?" Arya asked.

"Hmm, you may be right. Either way, we have to find some food," Blake said.

Krishna rubbed his fins across his belly. "I'm starving,"

"Well, there is one option," Sharktooth said. "We can travel to the deep part of the pond. Surely we can find food there!"

"But what about the koi?" Blake's voice trembled. "I don't want to get eaten by those fish. They scare me,"

"Don't be such a baby." Krishna puffed out his chest like a warrior. "We can outsmart the koi. I will lead the way!" He marched his fins back and forth like he was in the army.

By midafternoon, the betta fish decided to set out for their journey to the deepest part of the pond. Krishna sang the entire way.

"Krishna, you sound terrible," Arya complained. "That tune sounds like a whining donkey."

All the betta fish laughed.

Blake covered his ears with his fins. "I think Krishna is slowly going crazy from starvation. We need food!"

"At this point, I could eat anything, Fish food, bugs, an entire whale!" Arya laughed.

"We need to get serious. We're really far from home," Blake said.

Hours passed and the fish swam deeper and deeper. The sun had set, and a full moon rose on the horizon. Still, they swam further into the oblivion. The pond felt eerie with large shadows lurking in the distance.

"Guys, I have a bad feeling about this place," Krishna whispered.

"Look over there! It's the aerator," Blake said.

The aerator bubble and gurgled.

At that moment, a large shadow crept out from the depths revealing a massive koi fish in the moonlight. "Who goes there?" the koi asked in a deep, bellowing voice. "What business do you have in this part of the pond?" The koi dragged his tail on the bottom of the pond.

"We come in peace," Krishna said trembling.

"Food is scarce in the pond these days; we mean you no harm," Arya said.

"Hmm..." The koi considered their answers. "I haven't seen your kind in years. Betta fish are rare in these parts."

Suddenly, more and more koi fish crept into the moonlight. The betta fish were surrounded.

3

The Great Koi

"Don't eat us!" Blake swam behind Arya to hide.

"AAHAHAHAHA!" The koi laughed and encircled the betta fish. "Eat you? Eat you? AAHAHAHAHA!"

One koi swam forward and spoke. "We koi are vegetarians, not barbarians. We are the oldest and wisest fish in the pond." They all nodded their head at the same time.

"What a relief! The last thing I want to be is dinner for another fish. What's your name?" Krishna asked.

"My name is Ash. We koi have lived here for over 25 years. I have known the old man for a long time, since I was younger than you little betta fish." Ash replied.

"We have not seen him for three days. He has not come to the pond to feed us," Krishna said.

"Hmm, over the years his health has gotten worse. I hope nothing happened to my old friend," Ash said.

His tail continued to drag across the pond floor rocks.

Arya noticed a large object sticking out of Ash's tail. "Ash, you have a hook caught deep between the scales of your tail. You must be in so much pain. Can I try to remove it for you?"

"That would be fantastic," Ash replied in relief.

She swam behind him and grabbed it with her fins.

"It won't come out! Boy that's deep. Krishna come help me," Arya cried.

"ONE, TWO, THREE, PULL!" Arya pulled hard and with Krishna's help was able to free the hook from Ash's tail.

"Aahhh, that's a relief!" Ash swam in circles. "You fixed my tail. Thank you!" Ash

raised his fin summoning another koi fish. "I think you little fish will enjoy this," Ash said.

One of the smaller fish glided out from near the pond aerator carrying a large piece of food in her mouth. She dropped it before the betta fish.

"We make our own food from the plants that grow in the pond. Like I said before, we koi are vegetarians," Ash laughed.

"Eat to your heart's desire, my new friends," Ash announced. "Because of your kindness, we koi welcome you to stay with us".

That night was a great feast.

"See, Blake, the koi are not so scary after all," Sharktooth said.

"Ya, well they are still bigger than us," Blake replied with a mouth full of food.

"Hey, what are those koi fish doing over there near the aerator?" Krishna asked.

Six koi dancers grouped together and used the aerator as a stage, fins reaching high, tail fins spread, heads tilting back. The fish puffed out their chests while they swam in an elaborate circle. Deep bellowing drums played in the background while a crowd grew. Warm moonlight poured down

from above, fixing the dancers in a moment of suspension above the aerator. Bubbles ascended scattering the reflected moon glow across the depths of the pond floor like a disco ball.

"WOW, now that's cool," Arya said.

"We are celebrating the summer solstice. Since prehistoric times, the summer solstice has been seen as a significant time of year in many cultures, and has been marked by festivals and rituals. Dancing is how we koi celebrate," Ash replied.

The betta fish swam over to the stage and joined in the festivities.

They boogied down all night as the yellow pond lilies waved back and forth from the drums current. Finally, all the fish went to bed with a full belly.

"Ahh, now this is the life," Krishna murmured while drifting off to sleep.

The next morning the betta fish awoke to frantic shouting.

"RUN, HIDE!" Ash shouted.

Just then a fishing net plunged into the water and trapped the betta fish and koi.

4

Danger from Above

L ead weights of the net cut through the pond water striking the rocky floor. The latticework cinched tight around all of the betta fish and koi and began to lift out of the water.

"We are trapped! How will we escape?" Arya asked in a panic.

"Everyone hold your breath! We're approaching the surface of the pond," Ash ordered.

The net broke through the water and pulled the fish into the air. Hoisted above the rocky deck, Arya looked out and saw many people surrounding the little Japanese house. Construction workers were all over the place knocking down small buildings. Krishna peered through the net just in time to see the koi pond being drained.

Two people walked out of the house instructing another man who was wearing a construction hat. Krishna saw them walk by a real estate sign in the front yard with a large red sticker across it: *SOLD, New Construction Underway.*

"I think the old man moved away to go live with his children. You know, now that I think about it, he was having a really hard time moving around when he was feeding us. I did overhear his son asking him to come stay with them at their house a few weeks ago," Ash said.

Just then, the net containing all of the fish were heaved onto the back of a trailer and poured into a freshwater tank.

"PHEW!" Krishna exclaimed.

Arya gasped for breath. "Yeah, that was a close one guys."

Krishna saw a clipboard on the rusty trailer next to the tank. On the front were blueprints for a new house.

The truck started up and chugged down the road. There were potholes everywhere. The trailer bounced and bounced, spilling the water over every side of the tank.

"I think I am going to be sick," Krishna moaned. "Blaaahh." Krishna vomited everywhere.

"Yuck, that is so gross," Arya said.

One of the koi swam by and ate all the vomit.

"And that's even grosser!"

The betta fish laughed so hard they turned upside down in the tank.

Then all of the sudden, one of the construction men shouted, "STOP!" When the truck stopped, the man got out, walked back to the trailer and peered down at the tire. "The trailer has a flat tire."

The tall mountains loomed in the distance as the men gathered to inspect the damaged wheel.

"The tank is too heavy to pull on this pothole-infested dirt road," one of the construction men shouted.

"Hey, look over there," another of the men said.

Near the road, a turquoise-blue river wound its way through the mountain forest. Babbling and burbling, it sprung over the granite rocks in its way.

"Let's drop the fish in there to lighten the load," the construction worker shouted, as he pointed at the river. "They deserve better than to go back to the pet store. Plus, it's not worth all the headache".

The construction workers got out of the truck, unhooked the trailer, and backed up close to the river.

"This can't be good," Krishna said, as he looked out of the tank. "They are taking us to the river!"

5

River Rapids

"**A**lright men, ONE, TWO, THREE. PUSH!!" The construction men poured the tank into the river.

As the tank began to tip, Ash looked out toward the white rapids of the river. "Swim! Swim as hard as you can!" Ash grabbed the betta fish with his large fins and propelled them out of the tank with his broad and powerful tail.

SPLASH!

The water was cold, formed by the melted snow-capped mountains of the north.

"WOW, that's brisk! Krishna said, wrapping his fins around his entire body.

"Yikes!" Blake shouted as he saw Sharktooth floating upside-down.

Arya swam over as fast as she could against the current.

"Sharktooth, wake up!" Arya shook him back and forth till he opened his eyes.

Sharktooth slowly opened his eyes. "Woah, what a rush."

"What's that up ahead?" Blake screeched.

"It's a... it's a... WATERFALL!" Krishna shouted.

The betta fish swam as hard as they could but were unable to escape the powerful river current. The force of the rapids started to push them over the falls to the lagoon below.

"AHHHHHHH!" shouted all the betta fish in unison.

And then... silence.

Almost immediately, they all came to a sudden stop at the crest of the waterfall.

"Excuse me guys, the waterfall is only eight inches high. Look! My tail can touch the bottom while I just relax at the edge of the falls," Ash explained.

Krishna laughed. "Oh, well, this is a little embarrassing."

Blake opened his eyes and saw Ash towering over him with a great big grin on his face.

"See, there's nothing to be frightened of at all," Ash said. "You kids and your wild imaginations!"

More koi fish swam over the tiny waterfall waving at the betta fish as they passed by the brink hooting and hollering.

"Sometimes you just got to go with the flow, you know," said one of the koi as they passed by.

"It's downhill from here," said another.

"I FELL in love with the waterfall pretty rapidly," said a third koi as he laughed.

Arya and Krishna just rolled their eyes at the koi. "What a bunch of goofballs," Arya said.

Finally, the koi and betta fish regrouped downstream and headed south with the current. A galaxy of dragonflies buzzed through the musty air, wings shimmering in the sun. Krishna leapt from the water, catching one for a tasty dinner. "Yum! Those flies are delicious. Way better than fish pellets."

As they continued down the river, Arya discovered a group of rainbow trout in a shallow area where the river runs. "Hey guys, where are you heading?" she asked.

The rest of the betta fish and the koi also stopped to see what the trout had to say.

"Further downstream is Bass Lake," one trout explained. "We are going there for the mayflies. They are tasty this time of year. Want to join us?"

Now this school of fish was even larger. "Safety in numbers, I always say," Shark-tooth exclaimed.

The group continued to navigate the river. All of a sudden, four giant paws splashed down right in front of them, stirring up the silt from the riverbed.

"Lookout!" the trout screamed. "Swim for your life!"

6

Claws and Teeth

K rishna looked up while swimming between the gigantic paws. Long razor-sharp black claws flexed against the rocky river bed carving out trenches as they passed. "Now that's one ugly bear!" He chuckled. "Good luck catching me, you big snaggle toothed bear."

The grizzly peered down at Krishna. With his huge mouth open, the bear thrust his head into the water towards the little betta.

"He's going to get me!" Krishna found himself in the clutches of the bear. The river current pushed him closer to the bear's mouth and to his doom.

"Be brave!" Arya called after him.

Krishna wondered what he could do? An idea came to mind, but it would be dangerous. Instead of fighting the river current he used it to his advantage, but he'd have to swim faster than ever before. Krishna harnessed all his courage and strength and swam as fast has he could... into the jaws of the beast!

He dodged the beast's razor-sharp teeth as they closed around him. Krishna, with a burst of speed, escaped the perils of the bear by only a fraction of a second. The bear's jaws slammed shut - empty. Krishna swam away.

"You did it!" The betta fish surrounded Krishna, celebrating his escape.

Krishna looked back at the beast. "You're too slow to catch me old snaggletooth." Then he turned toward his friends. "Wahoo, let's go!!"

As the betta fish swam away together, the grizzly roared and faded into the distance.

"We have never seen a fish escape a bear's clutch. Wow! Now follow us. We have nearly reached the mayflies," one of the trout said.

The fish continued down the river, and the current finally began to calm.

Blake poked his head above the water surface and saw people standing alongside the riverbank. Smoke rose in the air from the campfires on land.

"Blake, get your head back in the water before someone sees you," Krishna said.

"Hey, I want to see too." Arya poked her head out of the water. She swam to the surface and saw that some people were fishing. Other people were hunched over panning for gold at the water's edge. If they only knew that there was a giant grizzly bear a few miles upstream perhaps they would be more cautious, she thought.

Ash was swimming with the school of trout as they passed by the humans. "You have got to be careful with those fishermen," one of the trout said to Ash. "People love to eat fish. My cousin was almost caught the last time we made the mayfly run in the spring."

Ash looked over at the betta fish concerned. "Hey guys, swim over here where I can see you."

The betta fish did as they were told, but on the way over, Arya felt a snag on her right fin. It was fishing net! She squirmed and squirmed, but the more she struggled to free herself from the net, the tighter it became around her tail.

"Help, Krishna! I am caught in the net!" Arya shouted.

Arya looked around and saw that all the fish were caught in the same net.

"Krishna! Krishna! Where are you?" Murky water engulfed the fish as the net became entangled around their fins. Arya could hear her friends cry out to each other for help, but there was nothing she could do to free them.

7

Land Ho!

"Pull! Pull! Come on gents, put your back into it!" a man cried.

As the fishnet rose from the water, Arya could see all the trout, koi, and finally betta fish caught in the mesh. The net was placed on the ground and the men sorted the catch into different buckets.

A young boy ran over. "Father, may I have those colorful fish?"

"Which ones, lad?"

"Those fish with the bright fins, may I have them?"

"Alright, Aaron," his father said with a smile. "Take your pick and put them in

your bucket. You worked hard today. You deserve it."

"Oh, thank you, father! I will take good care of them." Aaron reached down and picked up Arya, Krishna, Blake and Sharktooth. The young lad dropped the fish into his pail.

Arya swam to the surface, looked right at Aaron and whispered, "Hey kiddo, grab that fish over there in the net and bring him home, as well."

"Who said that?" asked the boy. He saw his father walking away from the river. "It must have been my Dad." The boy did as he was told and retrieved Ash from the large net and dropped him into the pail.

"Well, that's twice you helped me, Arya. I am in your debt. Now, how are we going to get out of this mess?" Ash asked.

Aaron picked up the pail and headed home. From inside the pail, Krishna gazed across the enchanted forest. The exquisiteness of the dusk's light had not yet launched to the lush, green leaves. Black shadows hung in the groves. Then a finger of supernatural light poked through the misty tree tops. It was followed by a whole loom of brightness, filtering down in seams of gold across the trail.

The rest of the fish surfaced to the top of the pail, oohing and awing in wonderment. Songbirds split the silence just as the forest flooded with warmth. Blake reached his fin out to feel the almond-brown tress, which stood serenely with a tender glow. Ash

took a breath to capture the aroma of the forest. A wave of harmony spread amongst the betta fish.

Aaron approached a house and looked down at his new friends in the pail. "I'll show you my family's house—your new home. You will love it."

The barn blossomed on the hill amid the grass and meadow flowers, as if it stood like an ancient tree weathered by time. Aaron, opened the russet-painted door adorned with its tired hinges that creaked and popped. The sweet musty odor of last winter's grain stores engulfed their senses.

Pails, tubs and tanks lined the barn walls, and tiny curious heads peeped out to investigate the disturbance.

"Aaron! It's time for supper," a woman called from the back porch.

"Coming, Mom," Aaron replied. He placed the pail on the dirt floor, raced out of the barn door, and slammed it shut behind him.

The betta fish poked their heads out of the pail and saw an unfamiliar set of eyes staring back at them.

The glistening eyes traced every movement of the betta fish. A large gray spade-like snout crept out from the shadowy dark, leaned forward with thick whisker-like barbels across his nose and mouth breaking the water's surface. With its sleek shape and rows of bony plates on its sides, it looked a bit like an armored torpedo. The water level in the bucket displaced and rippled from the shear mass of the creature's movement.

"What in the world is that?" Arya asked.

The giant continued to rise out of his bucket. Large scale-less pectoral fins revealed themselves.

"I do not like the look of this fish." Blake shuttered as he hid behind Ash with his head peeking out every few seconds.

Arya and Ash swam to the edge of their bucket with hesitant curiosity for the creature in the neighboring container. Arya lifted her head above the edge just in time to see the large pectoral fin flop down on her face.

"It's got me! HELP!" Arya shouted.

8

Buckets, Buckets Everywhere

Krishna swam with lightning speed, jumped out of the water and bit the large fin.

The sturgeon cried out, "Ouch! That really hurt. What did you do that for? I was just trying to say hello."

"You scared us. I thought you were a kraken by the way you were moving. Why didn't you just say hello like a normal fish?' Arya said.

"Well, I wasn't sure you all were friendly fish. Some of the fish in this barn aren't so nice. I wanted to make sure you were not like that," the sturgeon replied.

"What's your name?" Arya asked

The sturgeon leaned over his bucket and whispered, "They call me BATMAN!" He backed away laughing, "No, no, I'm just kidding. My name is Oscar, but I wish it was Batman. That would be way cooler."

Arya introduced all her friends to Oscar.

"What a day! Krishna, I cannot believe you bit Oscar. How are you holding up?" Sharktooth asked.

"My tummy hurts a little." Krishna turned to Oscar. "Sorry I bit you."

"All good bro, No worries. I am just happy to have some compadres. Hey man you look a little nauseous. You alright?" Oscar asked

"BURRRP! Boy, those dragonflies really gave me gas," Krishna said.

"Oh my gosh! Who belched in my presence?" A fish in a green bucket on the shelf shouted, "Yo, new fish, what's wrong with you? Were you raised in a barn?" His orange smooth-scaled head peered over the edge of his bucket. His large fins were draped over the side of the bucket.

"We're all living in a barn now!" Krishna laughed. "Hey, what's your name, crabby?"

"It's Gabe," the fish said. "Wait a minute, you guys are betta fish too! Who is that big cross-eyed fish with the giant head filling up your pail?"

"He is a koi," Arya replied.

"You better watch it small fry, don't make me come over there and rearrange your dorsal fin," shouted Ash.

A wave of water splashed out from another bucket,. "Oooo, a koi fish. I'm so special, big and tough, blah, blah blah," a catfish in the nearby tank mocked.

"You see, I told you that some of the fish in this barn are mean," Oscar said.

"Hey, stay out of this, you long-whiskered potato head," Gabe said to the catfish.

"Ooooohhh, I'm a big, tough betta fish. Look at me with my pretty colored fins," the catfish continued.

"That's it, potato head, I warned you!"

Arya and Krishna watched as Gabe jumped out of his water bucket, hit a burlap

sack on the wooden shelf, and then dove into their pail.

"Why on earth would you do that?' Krishna asked.

"Just watch..." Gabe giggled.

The sack began to sway, pouring into the catfish's tank. What came next was hilarious.

"What's in the sack?" Arya asked.

"That, my friends, is a big, stinking pile of cow manure. Hey catfish!" Gabe shouted. "Look up! Merry Christmas, you filthy animal!"

The green manure plopped into the tank. Fumes bubbled up to the surface with a putrid perfume of fermented cow dung as it broke apart and mixed with the water.

The catfish leaned his head over the side and screamed, "The smell! The smell! It's horrid! I am going to be sick!"

"Had enough?" Ash shouted.

"Yes, Yes, I want my Mommy. My apologies to all. Please help me escape this wretched cesspool."

"Okay, Okay, stop your whining, you big baby," Arya smirked. "You can come over to our pail."

Using all of his might, the catfish jumped out of his tank only to find that he was too heavy to fly through the air. He hit the side on the pail and plopped to the ground. All the fish in the barn gasped in horror as the catfish flipped and flopped on the ground.

9

Flying is for the Birds

The wide-eyed betta fish peered over the side of the pail.

"Hey Catfish, are you okay?" Arya asked.

There was no reply. The fish only flipped and flopped, flopped and flipped, until he was finally still.

"He's dead," Sharktooth whispered. "We killed that poor fish. If we would have left him alone, this would have never happened. We shouldn't have taunted him. It's all our fault!" Tears rolled down Sharktooth's face.

The betta fish were devastated as they turned their heads away.

"Just wait, he's a very clever catfish," Gabe said.

Suddenly the catfish bounced up "Aha! I got you good," he laughed and laughed and laughed. "You guys sure are so gullible, clearly you have never met a catfish before. Why, don't you know that catfish can live outside of water!"

"What? Who is this guy?" Arya asked in surprise. She watched the catfish dance around on the dirt floor of the barn like a ballerina. He was flipping his tail and flapping his fins.

"My name is Feo, the dancing catfish," Feo sang.

"See you gents later." He waddled and wiggled out the barn door into the meadow while singing "Hey Macarena...".

"Well now, I have never seen that in my life," Ash exclaimed.

All the fish in the barn started laughing so hard that they fell off the side of the pail into the water. Ten minutes later they heard a scream: "Ahh, HELP, get away from me you winged rat eater!"

Caw, Caw, A red-tailed hawk swooped down and clutched the catfish in his razor-sharp talons. His wings spread with the force of a hurricane, and the hawk took flight across the meadow. Mud and clay provided a safety buffer where the raptor's talons contacted the thick skin of his prey.

The betta fish could hear Feo the catfish in the distance. "Okay winged-rat, this is your final warning, put me down or feel the wrath of the MIGHTY catfish."

"CAW CAW," the hawk replied as he tried to peck at the fish.

Feo raised his right fin and wrapped it around the hawk's leg. Underneath Feo's fin was a large sharp spine loaded with poison, which he furiously jabbed into the hawk's leg, piercing his flesh.

"CAAAWWW." The Hawk cried out in pain and lost his grip on Feo.

Feo glided through the air, fins spread, piloting him to the safety of the lake. "Our paths will cross again betta fish," Feo shouted right before he plunged into the deep water.

"That was awesome! I guess he's a Flying Fish now," Krishna laughed.

"Feo is totally fearless. He's been like that since I met him," Gabe said.

"How did you end up in this barn Gabe?" Arya asked.

The betta fish and Ash swam near Gabe as he began to tell the story of how he arrived at the barn.

"Well, Feo and I had our own adventure. We have been in this barn for two months. Prior to this, I lived in a pet shop with my wife and two babies when one day a customer came in and purchased me. I tried to swim away but the fish net was too wide. My new owner took me to his house. For weeks I tried to think of a way to get back to my wife and babies. Don't get me wrong, my new owner was very nice, but I just couldn't stand the thought of never seeing my family again." Gabe said.

"Then what happened?" Krishna asked.

Gabe took a deep breath and the story continued, "I came up with a plan to escape. One afternoon my owner came home from work. He hung his hat in the closet and came over to my fish tank. While he watched me, I lay very still and was floating upside-down with my eyes closed."

"You played dead?" Arya asked.

"Yep, I faked my own death. My owner was upset and took me out of the tank. I held my breath for as long as I could while he walked over to the bathroom. Then he flushed me down the toilet." Gabe said with excitement. "I had escaped and was back on track to find my family."

"Oooohh, Gross. You swam in toilet water. I think I am going to be sick!" Sharktooth said.

"So how did you meet Feo?" Ash asked

Everyone looked at Gabe, "There I was, surfing the city sewer lines after being flushed down the toilet. The water current was strong and turbulent. I swam back and forth, navigating which pipe to choose. The closer I got to the light at the end of the line, the warmer the water grew. Then BOOM! I shot out of the sewer and landed in a nearby puddle, where I hit my head on a rock. When I woke up, Feo was shaking me and making sure I was okay. During the hot summer, the puddles dry up fast. Feo put me on his back and crawled toward a nearby stream. But we didn't make it. Aaron, the little boy who brought you all here, found us still on the ground and put us in a bucket of water. That's how we ended up in the barn.

"Now that's an adventure," Arya said

Ash looked over at Arya and Krishna swimming next to Gabe. "You know Gabe, Arya and Krishna look a lot like you."

Gabe's head shot up as he stared at Arya and Krishna. Then it dawned on him. He knew these little fish. "Kids?"

Krishna's and Arya's eyes grew big. "Papa?"

10

Reunited

"**K**ids, my babies, you have grown so much!" Gabe looked at Arya and Krishna and hugged them.

"We've missed you so much," Arya and Krishna replied.

"See, I knew it," Ash said. "Look at those three betta fish. They have the same color pattern and fin shape. I called it."

"This is unbelievable. I'm the luckiest fish alive. WAIT! Kids, now that we've found each other, we have to go find your mother," Gabe said.

"How in the world are we going to do that?" Arya asked

"First, we have to get out of this barn. But how? Hmmm," Krishna said.

Ash swam from side-to-side. A big smile spread across his face, "Betta fish, I have a plan".

Ash wrapped his large fins around the betta fish and began to disclose his plan.

Hours later...

That afternoon, Aaron skipped into the barn while humming, "Hey Macarena...". He had a burlap sack full of fish food. He stood over the tank. "Hi, my little fish friends, it's time for dinner."

Plop, plop the fish food hit the water.

Aaron looked down to watch the fish eat but to his surprise, Ash and the betta fish were at the water's surface staring back at him.

"Aaron, we need to talk," Blake said.

Aaron looked confused and shook his head, "Am I going crazy, did you just speak to me little fishy? Was that you who spoke to me at the river?".

"Arya is the fish that spoke to you at the river. You are not crazy Aaron. My

name is Blake. We need help. Can you help us?" Blake asked

Aaron blinked his eyes rapidly with his mouth wide open "Talking fish? Sure, I will help you. Tell me what to do."

"This is Arya and that little guy over there is Krishna," Blake stated. "They have to find their mother. We need you to convince your dad to take us to the city."

Blake and the rest of the fish told Aaron the entire story about how Gabe and his family became separated. Now, Arya and Krishna needed to go back to the city to find their mother.

After listening to the betta fish, Aaron agreed to help them. "It shouldn't be too hard," he said. "My dad is going to the city tomorrow to sell all of you."

"Aaron, it's time for supper. Your father is waiting," Aaron's mother cried out from the house front porch.

The next day, Aaron's father walked into the barn. He gathered all the tanks and placed them in his trunk. "I'm off to the city," he shouted.

"Father, wait. I want to come with you." Aaron ran up to his dad, "Thank you for helping me sell the fish. I want to be present and be a good business man like you someday." The boy winked at Ash and the betta fish who were watching from their tank.

"Great job, Aaron, thank you," Gabe whispered with a smile while winking back at him.

Aaron's father poured two other tanks of minnows into the betta fish's tank to save space in the truck. He then shut the tailgate and started driving down the dirt road.

"Not another car ride. I get car sick," Blake said, rubbing his belly. "Blaaah." Chunky green vomit filled the tank. Some of the small minnow fish began eating it.

"That's disgusting. It almost makes me want to Blaah." Krishna barfed all over Arya's tail.

Small minnow fish began nibbling the particles off her tail. "Gross!" Arya said.

The truck took a left turn and rumbled on down the highway. Traffic became heavy with sounds of honking and shouting.

"Ahh. The sounds of the city. How I missed them," Gabe said. "You never know what you might..." Gabe stared in silence as the murky water came to rest at the bottom of the tank. "What in the world..." He swam to the bottom to get a closer look.

"What is it?" Krishna asked.

"Why, it's a betta fish egg," Gabe explained.

11

Annie's Pet Shop

Gabe picked up the ruby color sphere and held it tightly in his fins.

"Hey, be careful with that egg. I've been carrying him for months," Blake said.

"What? Why didn't you say something before? How have you been carrying him?" Ash asked.

"I keep him tucked underneath my tail. I couldn't leave him in the koi pond all alone. I am sure he is a betta fish. Look at that ruby colored shell."

"Where did you find him in the koi pond?" Ash asked.

"The egg was at the very bottom of the pond. Sharktooth and I found him while playing. We didn't see his parents, so we decided to care for him. We even named him: Shivam. It is an auspicious name for someone who brings good luck. After that, we met all of you guys, and here we are, one big happy family on an adventure."

"Aw, he's so cute," said Arya and Krishna at the same time.

The songs of the city hummed in the background and grew louder as the truck neared the metropolis.

The fish felt the truck come to a screeching stop. "We have arrived," Gabe said.

The trunk opened and Aaron inspected the tank. The fish looked out and saw the sign over the entrance door: *Annie's Pet Shop*.

"Great plan, Ash. It was a good idea to get Aaron to help us. I hope we can find my mom here in the shop," Krishna said.

Ding, Ding chimed the door. Aaron and his father walked into the pet shop.

"Greetings and welcome to Annie's Pet Shop. I am Annie. We have the finest collection of unique pets. Browse at your leisure gentlemen," the owner announced.

"Ma'am, we are here to sell," Aaron replied. Would you be interested in inspecting our stock?"

Annie stepped out onto the street, strolled over to the truck and tapped on the tank.

"There's a long-haired lady tapping on the tank," Krishna said.

Annie peered into the tank. "Well, these are interesting specimens. I will take all of them." She called out to an employee inside the shop. "Amer, Amer, AMER! Come out and help us carry the tank inside."

"Coming ma'am," Amer replied.

Aaron looked down at the fish with tears welling up around his eyes, "I really liked taking care of all of you. Good luck finding your mother. I will miss y'all."

"Thank you, Aaron, for helping us. Great job getting back to the city. We will meet again someday," Gabe said.

Arya and Krishna looked at the pet shop through the fish tank glass. "This place sure has a lot of animals" Krishna said.

"Yeah, I bet we will make all kinds of friends," Arya said.

"Look over there, it's a group of bearded dragon lizards!" Blake shouted with excitement.

Gabe swam over holding Shivam, the egg. "I think we need to build a place to sleep at night. You never know what other fish could be dropped into our tank tomorrow."

The betta fish and Ash worked quickly to move stones from the bottom of the tank. They stacked pebbles on top of each other until the castle was complete. The main entrance was a labyrinth of caves built to confuse any other fish who may wish to trespass. It was exhausting work, but well worth the effort.

Krishna yawned. "Time for bed guys, let's call it a day."

The fish snuggled up inside the rock castle and drifted off to sleep.

The next morning, the sun rose in the east breaking through the horizon. Shimmering beams of blue, tangerine and apricot colors filled the sky as the morning dew evaporated away from the pet shops glass windows. The pet shop came alive as all the animals awoke from their slumber.

"Good morning, fellow creatures," Krishna said.

Arya was already swimming at the far end of the tank near the filtration system that flowed like a waterfall. Peering back at her was an old alligator and a snapping turtle.

"Those are some brightly color fins you have little one. What's your name?" the turtle asked.

"I am Arya, and that is Krishna, Blake, Sharktooth, Ash, and my dad Gabe," she said pointing out the others. "Oh, and that egg is Shivam. He hasn't hatched yet."

"I am Kobe. I've been living in this shop for years. I have seen many animals come and go."

"Are the humans nice?" Arya asked.

"Amer, the manager, is very nice. You can trust him. He always takes good care of us," Kobe replied.

Just then, Amer unlocked the front door of the shop and stepped in. "Good morning, everyone." He picked up a bag of fish food. "Who's hungry?" Amer asked, making his rounds from tank to tank.

Plop, plop went the fish pellets. Gabe and the rest of the fish swam to the surface to enjoy their breakfast.

"Not bad at all. Here, try the green pellets guys," Ash said, munching on the food.

Just then, a postwoman left a box outside the front door. "Looks like we have our first delivery of the day," Amer said.

He walked over, grabbed the box and sat it on the counter. He opened the package near the fish tank. "Well now, what do we have here? Why, it's more betta fish. I remember Annie ordering them last week."

Then he took out the container, opened the lid, and poured the fish into the tank.

12
New Friends

Krishna suddenly looked up. "What in world? Incoming! Who are you guys? Hurry, swim to the castle," he said to his friends. "Go, Go, Go!"

"SWIM for cover!" Ash shouted.

"Blake, Sharktooth, get to the fortress," Gabe instructed. He grabbed Shivam and tucked him under his right fin like a football. "Find cover."

All the fish hid in the fortress, peeking their heads out the window from time to time.

Two small bright red betta fish swam up to the castle where the rest were hiding. They each had a purple streak of scales on their tail.

"Wait, wait, Stop! We just want to be friends. I am Surya and this is my little sister Sanya," said Surya.

"What's up, Dudes!" Sanya shouted.

"You guys are not scary at all," said Krishna as he poked his head out of the castle window. "You are small betta fish just like us."

Ash and the rest of the betta fish came out of the castle.

Amer looked down, observing the fish in astonishment. "This is utterly amazing. These fish are communicating with each other," he thought. Amer grabbed a chair and sat next to the tank.

While Krishna and Sanya were having their conversation, Amer tapped on the glass. "Can you fish understand me?' Amer asked.

Sanya turned around and nodded her head at Amer and then shooed him away with her fin. "The man was eavesdropping, how rude."

"I must be going crazy." Amer rubbed his eyes and looked closer. "They are going to ship me off to the crazy house. No one would ever believe me if I told them I could communicate with fish."

Arya swam to the surface, making eye contact with Amer. "Hey, what's a crazy house?"

"You can TALK !?!?!" Amer's eyes crossed, and he let out a sigh as he fell from his chair down to the floor with a thud.

"Timber!" Surya shouted.

"He's passed out cold," Gabe said.

"People never knew that fish could talk. No wonder Amer freaked out." Ash said.

"I am sure he is going to wake up with a pounding headache." Arya said.

"I guess it was going to happen eventually" Ash declared.

Five minutes later, Amer slowly opened his eyes and pulled himself up off the wood floor. "I must have hit my head," he whispered in a drowsy voice.

"Hey Amer. Over here. You passed out like a little baby," Surya said.

"Ya, like a baby." Sanya laughed and giggled.

Amer rubbed his head. "I've been working too hard." He locked up the shop and called Annie on the phone.

"Hello? Annie, can you cover for me at the shop? I am not feeling well. I need to go home and rest." He listened to Annie's response. "Okay, thank you, Annie."

Arya turned to the other fish. "I think we can trust Amer, he is a good guy."

"There is nothing wrong with talking to humans, you just have to be a little careful about whom you speak to" Sharktooth proclaimed.

"I agree" said Arya.

"No one will believe him. Amer said it himself. People will think he's gone mad. Besides, it might just be our ticket out of this place," Krishna said.

Pop. Crack. Shivam began to move around inside the egg. Then the egg went still.

"Look, that egg is going to hatch soon," Arya said. "We all need to stick together. I think that if we keep talking to Amer, he will be our friend."

"Guys, I have an idea," Gabe said. "It will take a little faith, and we may need to break some rules, but it should work."

13

Ring, Ring Went the Register. Sold!

The next day, Amer watched nervously from the cash register as two children in school uniforms stared at the betta fish.

The kids tapped on the glass. "Here fishy fishy! Mom, can we get a fish? I like the orange one," the boy said.

"Maybe next time, dear," the mom replied. "Come along now. We have to stop by the grocery store on the way home."

As soon as the kids left, Gabe called the fish into a huddle. "Here's the plan, squad. We have to talk to Amer and explain why we need to stay together. We need a human friend."

Ash and all the betta fish agreed.

Amer looked up at the clock: 6:00pm. Closing time. He took a deep breath and let out a sigh of relief that no customers bought the fish. Amer locked the front door and walked over to Arya. "I bet you guys would all want to stay together?"

Arya nodded her head yes.

Surya swam to the top of the fish tank. "Excuse me, Mr. Amer, sir. We have to stick together. Little baby Shivam is going to hatch soon and we have to take care of him."

"Take a look, Amer." Gabe held up the egg.

Looking at the fish, Amer stepped back for a moment to think. "I need to help these betta fish." Then the idea came to him in a flash of bursting thought. He smiled and turned to face the fish.

"Would you all like to come home with me?" Amer asked.

"Yes. On one condition: you can never let anyone know that we can talk. Only we get to choose which humans are safe to speak to," Arya said.

"It's a deal," said Amer.

Amer turned away and opened the drawer of the cash register. DING went the drawer. "That will be $97.50," he said out loud to himself. He took money from his wallet to pay for the fish and put it into the drawer. The drawer shut with a bang.

Krishna watched as Amer picked up the fish tank. "Come on guys, you're coming home with me. You guys are special. I will keep you safe."

Ash swam around the tank and looked out the window as they walked down the city sidewalk. "This place is a concrete jungle. Look over there, it's a Sushi restaurant. I bet there are all kinds of fish there."

"Are you crazy? That's where they serve fish to eat. You'd be on the menu, served with wasabi and ginger," said Surya.

"They'd make you into a koi sushi role," Sanya said, laughing.

"Ha, ha." Ash laughed with his friends. "I would definitely give one of those humans indigestion."

After another couple blocks, Amer entered an apartment building. "We are here little ones," he said. Tall concrete columns framed the twenty-foot-high arched windows at the entrance. Amer walked through the lobby to the elevator doors.

Ding! The doors opened and Amer walked into the elevator.

"What floor, sir?" the elevator operator asked.

"Twenty-third floor, please."

The elevator shot up like a bullet.

"Twenty third floor sir," said the elevator operator.

Amer stepped out and walked down the hallway to his apartment.

The key slid into the deadbolt, the lock clicked and then twisted, and the door swung open. Amer pushed through the door and set the fish tank on the hand-carved walnut coffee table near the window.

"That tank sure is heavy. Welcome home my friends," Amer said.

"Wow, love the apartment. Very nice," Gabe said.

"Nice view!" Sharktooth said.

Ash stretched his fins and relaxed on the bottom of the fish tank. "Home sweet home".

"What do you guys want to do?" Amer asked.

Sanya swam up to the top of the tank. "Can we go to the beach? I have always wanted to see the ocean and smell the salty air."

Amer thought for a moment. "Well, tomorrow is my day off from work," he said. "It's been a while since I had a break. Yes, I'd love to go, great idea!"

"Wahoo!" Surya cried out.

"Amer, Amer! Don't you want to bring a friend? Maybe a girlfriend?" Surya asked.

"Well, there is something I have wanted to do for a while," Amer stated. He pulled out his cell phone and pushed some buttons. "Hello, Annie? Hi, it's Amer. I was wondering if you wanted to come to the beach with me and a few of my new friends?"

The fish waited as Amer fell silent and listened to Annie's answer.

"I would love to come, what took you so long to ask me to go do something outside of work. I will pack my bags tonight." Annie said.

"Oh, that's wonderful, Annie!" Amer winked at the fish. "Come to my apartment morning at nine." He hung up the phone with a huge smile on his face.

"OOoooohh," whispered Sanya. "Amer has a girlfriend."

Amer blushed. "Time for bed, little ones." He walked over and turned out the lights.

"He's right," Gabe said. "We'll need a good night sleep for the beach."

"I can't sleep," Sharktooth said. "Too excited!" He zoomed around the fish tank.

"Can we go surfing?' Blake asked.

"You can do whatever you want as long as you go to sleep now, please," Ash said with a grumpy voice. "Good night."

"Time for another adventure," Arya mumbled as she drifted off to sleep.

14

Hang Ten, Dude!

Early the next morning, Amer packed a bag with all his stuff and plenty of fish food. He loaded his car, placing the fish tank in the back of the car.

Annie arrived, promptly at nine, at the apartment building lobby. "Hi Amer, I am ready to go."

"Hey, love birds, let's get this car moving. I want to get a tan!" Sanya giggled.

"Oh, my!" Annie exclaimed. "Did that fish just speak to us?"

Amer took a breath. "I will explain on the way to the beach."

"Alright, we are off to the beach!" Blake shouted excitedly.

After a two-hour car ride, they reached the coast. Amer told Annie the entire story about the fish along the way.

"I think they are wonder fish. I never knew that fish could talk," said Annie.

Seagulls cawed as they parked the car and got out. Amer went to the back, picked up the tank and headed for the beach. Annie carried the towels and beach umbrella.

The sound of crashing waves grew louder as they walked toward the marble white sand. They headed closer to the surf. The salty wind pressed against Krishna's face.

"Annie, I'm really glad you came with us," Amer said. "Guys, you can trust Annie. She will help me look after you," Amer said to the betta fish.

Krishna swam to the top of the fish tank, peered into Annie's big brown eyes and said, "Hello."

Annie looked in astonishment at Krishna. "I am still amazed you fish can talk! How did you learn to speak? Amer, did you teach them?"

"No, they could already speak when I found them," Amer replied.

Ash looked at both of the humans. "Animals have always been able to speak. We start learning when we're babies, just like you. That's one of the many reasons why we need to be here for Shivam when he hatches."

"But Annie," Amer interrupted, "You must promise to keep this a secret. The fish are very selective when speaking to humans. I have no idea why they chose to speak to me and now to you."

Annie looked at Amer. "Maybe the betta fish trust you because you have a kind and gentle soul."

"Amer, can you place our fish tank in the shallow waves?" Surya asked "I want to see all the salt water fish."

Amer thought about it for a moment. Would it be safe?

"Please, please, please Amer." Sanya begged as she acted like a tiny whale breaching and squirting water out of her mouth.

"Okay, okay, just be careful," Amer said.

Amer walked close to the surf where the waves were breaking against the sand and placed the fish tank on the beach.

The low tide waves gently kissed the tank's glass. Ash and the betta fish looked in sheer wonder at the marine life.

"Look, a starfish!" Blake exclaimed.

A school of mackerel blazed by the tank, their silver scales reflecting the sunlight.

"I think they are just as curious about us as we are about them," Ash declared.

One by one, small hermit crabs surrounded the exterior of the fish tank, searching for food in the sand.

"Guys, check this out!" Gabe gasped. "Those waves are coming right for us!"

"Take cover!" Arya shouted.

The waves splashed right in front of the tank, spraying sea foam against the glass. The foam melted away leaving a residue on the glass.

"Now that was cool," Blake said.

The waves grew higher and higher as the tide rose.

"This is crazy. Look, there goes a seahorse, and there's a starfish climbing the tank. Look at those suckers pressed against the glass," Surya said.

Sanya held baby Shivam (who was still an egg) and showed him the marine life swimming around the tank.

An hour passed by as the squad enjoyed all the wonders of ocean life.

Amer had left the betta fish in the swash while he and Annie made a picnic on the beach. Mesmerized by Annie, he had completely forgotten about his little friends.

"You know, guys, those waves are getting a little higher," Krishna said. "Where are Amer and Annie? I think they need to move us closer to shore. The tide is rising."

Blake swam to the edge of the tank. He saw Amer and Annie laughing and having a picnic on the beach. "Guys, I think we need to get their attention".

The fish grouped together and shouted in unison, "HELP! Hey, you need to move us! Help, Amer! Annie, over here!"

The sound of the wind, surf and crashing waves drowned out their cry for help. The fish tank now shook with every crashing wave. It wobbled and started to float as the riptide began to pull them out to sea.

"Look out!" Surya shouted.

15

Briny Water

An ocean wave had risen high enough to spill into the top of the tank.

"What's the big deal?" Arya asked.

"It's salt water," Sanya explained. "We can only survive in fresh water. What do we do?"

The smell of salt became pungent in the fresh water fish tank.

Arya could feel the salt water choking her gills. She swam to the top of the tank and shouted with all her breath, "Amer, HELP US!"

Thankfully, Amer heard her and saw the ocean waves flooding the fish tank. "Oh, my goodness. I am coming my friends!"

"Amer better hurry. I don't know how long we can last in briny water. This salt water burns my gills," Ash said.

By the time Amer reached the tank, all the fish were struggling to breathe. Amer knew he had to find fresh water fast or his friends would never survive.

"Amer! Across the street in the shopping center! We have to hurry!" Annie shouted, pointing to an aquarium store in the shopping center.

"Hold on guys!" Amer said worriedly. He picked up the tank and raced to the aquarium store.

Krishna looked up at Amer just as everything faded to black and he passed out.

Amer rushed into the store.

"Can I help you, sir?" the clerk asked.

"I need fresh water! My fish are going to die. Please hand me that fish net".

The clerk ran over to Amer and scooped out all the fish from the contaminated tank. The betta fish and Ash were not moving. "I hope this works," the clerk said. She gently placed all the fish into a clean fresh water tank in the store.

"Come on, come on! Guys, you can't leave me. It's all my fault," Amer cried. He placed his hand in the tank and carefully moved the fish around, allowing fresh water to flow through their gills.

Annie helped Amer move the fish around the tank.

Arya's tail began to move. Krishna opened his eyes. Surya, Sanya, Ash, Gabe, Blake and Sharktooth started to shake their fins. Amer watched with a sigh of relief.

All of the sudden, a fish shouted from her underwater cave. "What in the world is going on out here? Who is in my fish tank and why does it stink of salt water? "

Arya looked around. "This fish tank looks so familiar to me," she said. "I feel like we have been here before, Krishna."

"This cave... could it be...? Yes, kids it's our old home from when you were babies!" Gabe shouted.

"The voice from the cave, I've heard it before," Krishna said. Without thinking, he quickly swam into the glass cave. All the betta fish bravely followed him.

"Hello, who is in here?" Sanya echoed.

A fish swam out into the light. She had bright red fins and a long tail. She stared at the betta fish. "Krishna, Arya, Gabe... is that you? It's been so long. Last time we saw each other, you kids had just hatched from an egg. Then you and your sister were sent to the koi pond.

Gabe, Krishna, and Arya recognized the voice. They could barely believe their eyes and ears...

"Mama?" Krishna's voice shook with anticipation.

"Yes," the red-finned fish said. "It's me, your mother. I missed you all so much. Now we're finally all together!" Amita said.

Amita swam over to Gabe, Krishna and Arya. She gave them a hug. All the fish were so happy to be together.

Amita looked up at Amer with a puzzled face.

16

Home Sweet Home

Amita looked up at Amer and Annie, "Who are they?"

"Oh, those are our friends. They can be trusted. Yes, they know we can talk, but our secret is safe with them," Gabe said.

"Well okay, but it will take a little getting used to, communicating with humans," Amita said.

Amer and Annie waved at all the fish. Annie looked behind her and saw that the store clerk was distracted helping another customer.

"Mama, what happened to you?" Arya asked.

All the fish, Amer and Annie huddled around to listen to Amita.

"After Gabe was sold to a new owner, I was so worried that Arya and Krishna would be next. I hid them deep in the glass cave so that no one would find them. A few weeks after Gabe was sold, I was out getting food for the kids from the surface of the tank when a couple walked into the pet shop and stopped right in front of my fish tank. I saw them look at me and then call the clerk over. She had a net. I swam as fast as I could to the cave but the net scooped me up."

"Were you scared, Mama?" Krishna asked.

"Yes, I did not want to leave my babies," Amita hugged Krishna and Arya tightly.

Amita swam in front of all the fish, "I had dropped all the food in front of the cave for the kids. It was the best I could do. They lifted me out of the tank. I was so worried about my babies. I thought I would never see them again. My new owners were very nice and the fish tank they had was beautiful. After they fed me, I settled in for the night and started thinking of a plan to get back to the shop."

"What happed next?" Sanya asked.

"That night was the scariest night of my life. The couple also owned a CAT!" Amita said.

"A cat? Oh no! What happened?" Krishna asked.

Amita took a deep breath. "I was swimming around trying to see if I could jump out of the fish tank and swim down the sink drain to escape, when I looked up and saw a white and gray cat paw slosh around in the fish tank."

"The cat hissed and meowed while trying to catch me". Amita's voice trailed.

"Yikes!" Arya scurried closer to her mother.

"I ducked and dove to escape the sharp clawed paws," Amita said. "But after a while I got tired. The cat finally had me cornered in the fish tank. Just as things were going black, the light in the room turned on. My owner shooed away the mean old cat and brought my fish tank into the bedroom to keep me safe for the rest of the night. The next day, I heard the couple debating about whether to keep me or the cat. I think the cat won because that afternoon they returned me to the pet store."

"You missed us by only a few hours, Mama," Krishna said

"When the couple returned me, I was overjoyed to be home. I swam down to the cave in our fish tank. I looked for you kids and cried out but no one was there. It was one of the hardest days of my life," Amita said.

"We were gone by then, Mama. Krishna had swam out of the cave to get the food in the front entrance. We looked for you all over the place and that's when the old man saw us and took Krishna and I to his koi pond," Arya explained.

"We were excited about going on an adventure, maybe, I think, because deep down, we knew we would find you and dad," Krishna said.

"Well, we are back now," Arya said. She reached out to hug her mother. Gabe and Krishna joined in for a tight family hug.

Ash, Surya, Sanya, Blake, Sharktooth and Sanya (who was still holding Shivam)

joined in as well. "We did it Krishna! We found our family," Arya cried.

Amer walked over to the cash register. "Hello clerk, I would like to buy that red-finned betta fish please."

DING went the cash register.

Stay tuned for the next book...

Discussion Questions

1. Where did the name "betta fish" come from?
2. Where do betta fish originate?
3. What is summer solstice?
4. Can fish talk?
5. When did people start keeping betta fish as pets?

For answers to these questions and more, please visit our website
www.bettafishadventures.com

Made in the USA
Columbia, SC
14 February 2022